This book belongs to

_____

Grammy, will you?

Phyllis Larson

Order this book online at www.trafford.com
or email orders@trafford.com

Most Trafford titles are also available at major online book retailers.

Printed in Victoria, BC, Canada.

ISBN: 978-1-4269-2299-2 (SC)

Our mission is to efficiently provide the world's finest, most comprehensive book publishing service, enabling every author to experience success. To find out how to publish your book, your way, and have it available worldwide, visit us online at www.trafford.com

Trafford rev. 12/17/2009

www.trafford.com

North America & international
toll-free: 1 888 232 4444 (USA & Canada)
phone: 250 383 6864 ♦ fax: 812 355 4082

I lovingly dedicate this book
to all my grandchildren,
whom I cherish,
and to Almighty God
in gratitude for the precious time
he is allowing me to be with them.

Grammy, will you play with me?
You can sit next to my dolly.
I'll make you some tea.

Grammy, will you read me a book?
I like that one
About the elephant and a mouse.
Grammy, when can I come to your house?

Grammy, will you snuggle with me?
Sure, we can both fit in this chair,
You'll see.
I'll share my blanket with you, too.
It's my favorite. Do you remember
That I got it from you?

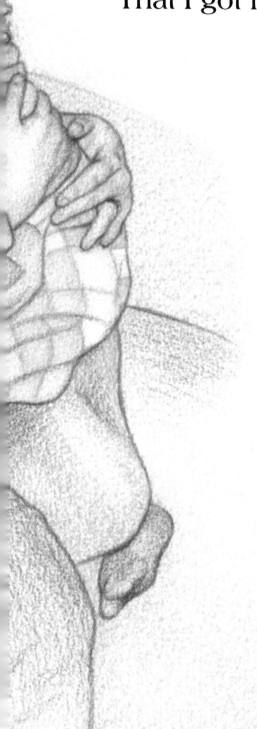

Grammy, will you sit with me
While I take my bath?
Watch me throw this sponge thru the net.
That's OK, Mommy doesn't mind
If I get the floor wet.

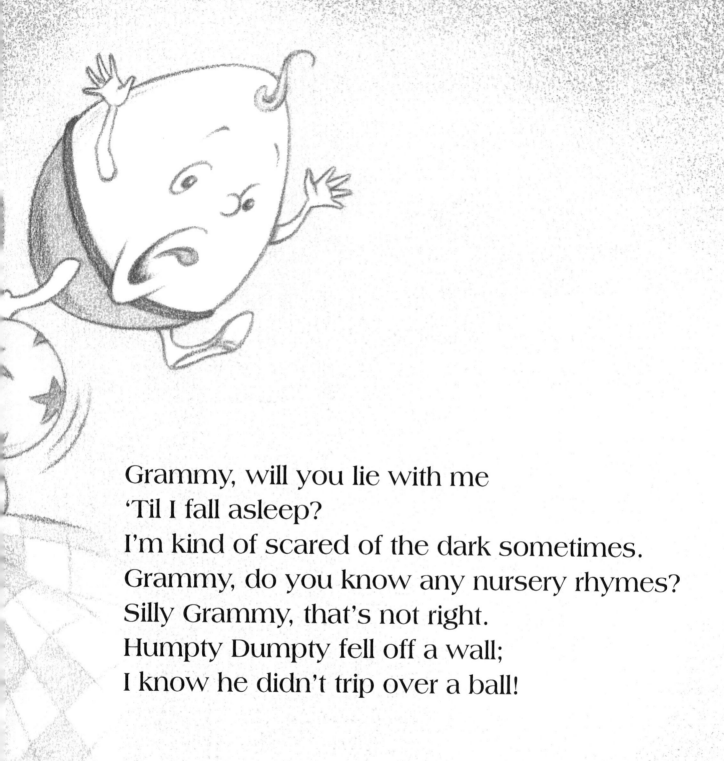

Grammy, will you lie with me
'Til I fall asleep?
I'm kind of scared of the dark sometimes.
Grammy, do you know any nursery rhymes?
Silly Grammy, that's not right.
Humpty Dumpty fell off a wall;
I know he didn't trip over a ball!

Grammy, will you be here in the morning
When I wake up?
I don't want you to go.
Grammy, will you get me some water in a cup?

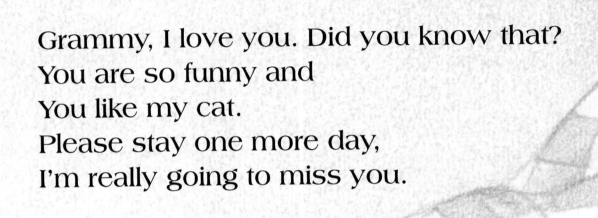

Grammy, I love you. Did you know that?
You are so funny and
You like my cat.
Please stay one more day,
I'm really going to miss you.

Please...Oh please, Grammy, will you?

Made in the USA
Lexington, KY
07 July 2015